MAX E. JAMES

FISHING FEVER

J. RYAN HERSEY

Illustrated by Gustavo Mazali

TABLE OF CONTENTS

To my boys – May you remember and laugh
as you read to your future children.

FREE DOWNLOAD

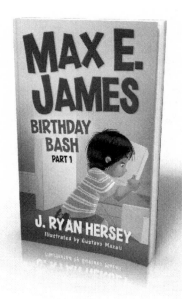

Will Max's one and only birthday wish come true?

Join my Kids' Club to get your free copy of the second book in the Max E. James children's series. Type the link below into your browser to get started.

http://eepurl.com/cfcfkj

CHAPTER 1

The Operation

SCRATCH. SCRATCH.

I sat up and rubbed my eyes. Today was the day our training would finally pay off. I could feel it. I swung my feet over the side of the bed.

Scratch. Scratch.

"Hold on a second," I said. "Where'd I put my whistle?"

I slipped off the bed and landed on something squishy.

"Eewh," I said. "What is that?"

I shut my eyes and crossed my fingers. Please don't stick, please don't stick. I shook my feet and a mangled clump of fluff and fur dropped to the floor.

"No, puppy!" I said. "That's the third stuffed animal this week. I can't even tell who it is!"

I scowled at my little white dog, Birthday Miracle, and tossed the slobbery mess she'd made into the trash.

"I won't even bother burying this one since you'll just dig it up. Then I'll have to wipe up your little mud tracks when you drag it through the house."

Birthday Miracle wagged her tail and scratched the door again.

"Hold on a second. You need monster protection."

I slung my favorite blanket, Fuzzy, around Birthday Miracle's neck. She wiggled, but I still managed to tie a loose knot.

"That will have to do," I said. "Now it's time for 'Operation Attack Cody'."

I admired my handiwork and grabbed my whistle.

"Remember," I said. "Just like we practiced."

Birthday Miracle nibbled at Fuzzy as I poked my head out the door.

"No movement in the hall," I whispered, "and I can hear the TV, so Cody's already out there. Ready?"

Birthday Miracle tilted her head and yawned.

"One. Two. Three!" I flung the door open and blew the whistle as hard as I could.

Tweeeeet!

"Sic 'em!" I screamed.

Birthday Miracle scurried down the hall with her blanket-cape trailing behind.

I slammed the door, counted to five, then listened for Cody's cries as 'Operation Attack Cody' began.

By now, I imagined that her needle teeth would be digging into Cody's arms. Where was the screaming? The crying?

"Hmm. It's too quiet. I should have heard something by now."

I popped my head out the door and blew the whistle again.

Tweeeeet! Tweeeeet!

"Attack!" I called into the darkness.

I had to see for myself, so I raced into the living room. I turned the corner and there was Cody, calmly watching TV.

"What?!" I said.

Birthday Miracle was sitting on his lap, licking his face! She hadn't bared a single needle tooth!

Tweeeeet! Tweeeeet!

"There's no licking in this operation, Birthday Miracle!" I ordered.

Cody laughed.

"Stop tying your blanket around that dog," he said. "She trips over it."

"Fuzzy was an important part of the operation," I said. "Do you see any monsters?"

"Great operation," Cody said shaking his head.

Birthday Miracle whined and jumped off the couch. She strutted down the hall into the darkness, with Fuzzy trailing close behind.

I clenched my teeth. "There's always next time."

"And another thing," he said. "You'd better

stop blowing that whistle. You're going to wake up Mommy and Daddy."

"What? My training whistle?" I spun it around in the air. "Mommy loves this thing. She tried to keep it for herself."

Cody looked at me funny.

"I brought it home last week and it disappeared the same day," I said. "You know where I finally found it?"

"Where? In the trash can?"

"Nope! I found it in her makeup box. The one on the really high shelf. I'm telling you, she wants it for herself."

I stared at the whistle. "Anyway, now I'm using it to train Birthday Miracle."

"I see that's going well," Cody said.

A door creaked and someone stumbled into the hall.

"Ahhhh!" It was Daddy. His voice echoed down the hall. "Gross!" he said. "The floor is wet!"

Cody glared at me. "Did you let the dog out?"

CHAPTER 2

The Legend of Toothy Brutus

"One responsibility," Daddy mumbled. "Just one. You don't have to feed or bathe her. Even Mommy usually gets stuck walking her."

"Uh-oh," Cody said. "He's talking to himself again."

We tiptoed to the hall for a peek. There he was, balancing on one foot. We lost it.

"'Please, Daddy'," he said in a squeaky kid voice. "'We'll take care of a puppy. We promise. We'll do anything.'"

We tried to hold it in, but we couldn't stop laughing. My belly began to hurt.

"That's what I get for listening to you boys." Daddy looked up at us. "Would somebody please

get me a paper towel? And for goodness' sake, let the dog out!"

"By the looks of it, she doesn't have to go anymore," said Cody.

I snickered, but Daddy didn't. Cody let the dog out and I went to the kitchen to grab some paper towels.

Mommy was awake when I returned. She was standing beside Daddy.

"So where'd he go, Max?" she asked.

"Where'd who go?" I said.

"The angry little traffic cop who kept blowing his whistle," she said, leaning closer. "My children certainly wouldn't do a thing like that. So, I figure there's a tiny policeman roaming the house somewhere."

I grinned but didn't say a word.

She held out her hand. "Please turn in your whistle, Officer."

"But I just got it back!" I said.

She glared at me.

I reluctantly handed the whistle to her.

"Come on," she said. "Let's get breakfast going while Daddy finishes tidying up."

"Thanks for the hand, Mommy," Daddy said.

She smiled. "You're doing just fine, honey."

I set the table and Mommy filled two bowls with cereal. I lifted the first scoop to my mouth and almost choked on it when Cody burst through the door.

"They're here!" he shouted. He ran in and slammed a long rectangular box on the table.

"They weren't supposed to come until next week," he said. He slashed the cardboard box with a pair of scissors.

"Careful with those," Mommy said.

"What?" I asked. "What's in the box?"

The packing paper fell away and revealed two shiny fishing rods.

"These," he said.

He handed me one. I turned the crank.

Click. Click. Click.

Daddy appeared with a handful of dirty paper towels. "Whoa," he said. "Nice poles. I see they came early."

"Please tell us the story again," I said, stuffing another spoonful of cereal in my mouth.

"Aren't you tired of that story yet?" He asked.

"Are you kidding me?" Cody said. "It's our favorite!"

"Well," he said. "They call him Toothy Brutus. Some say he's named after his huge set of choppers. Some say he's named after his brute strength. Many have tried but he's never been caught. They say he snaps your line if—"

"Or even your pole, right?" Cody said.

"Yes," Daddy said. "He can even snap your pole if you're lucky enough to hook him. When I was your age, I was fishing alone and already had a few trout on the stringer when I started packing up."

"That's when you heard it, right?" I said.

Daddy pulled a chair up to the table. "Yes," he said. "It reminded me of a whip cracking or a huge mouse-trap snapping."

You could hear a pin drop in the kitchen.

"I turned to see what it was, but all I saw were a few ripples in the water. I had nothing to lose, so I baited my hook and tossed it out."

I looked at Cody and scooted my chair closer. "I love this part."

"As soon as it landed," Daddy said, "the hook and bobber disappeared in a splash."

"Then what?" Cody asked.

"My pole bent over so far the tip touched the water. Line began peeling off the reel and it almost pulled me in."

Cody swallowed. "But you held on, right? You had a good grip?"

"Yes," Daddy said. "But Toothy Brutus was so strong and swam so fast that he stripped all the line off the reel in just a few seconds."

We finished breakfast in silence, soaking it all in. I wondered what kind of fish could do that and how big it must be all these years later.

"What do you think it is?" I said.

"I don't know," Daddy said. "I never saw it."

"I bet it's a catfish," Cody said. "Or a large-mouth bass."

"What if it's not a fish at all?" I suggested.

Cody looked puzzled.

"What if it's a pet that got flushed down the toilet? Like a mutant goldfish or a little alligator that's three-hundred-feet long now."

I stretched my arms out as far as I could.

"Yeah," said Cody, "or maybe it's the Loch Ness Monster."

My eyes widened and my mouth dropped open.

"Maybe!" I said.

"No, gentlemen," said Daddy. "It's not any of those things. Just a big sneaky fish that hasn't been caught yet."

"How do you know?" I asked. "You just said you didn't see it."

"Wait a second," Cody said. "Our poles came early, so can we go fishing today?"

"Yeah!" I said. "Please, Daddy. Can we?"

CHAPTER 3

Wiggly Worm Party

MY HEART POUNDED while we waited for the answer. I glanced at Cody, whose eyes were shut tight in concentration.

"Hmm," Daddy said, "I don't think so."

"But, but, why not?" I said.

"Because, sillies. We don't have any bait."

"Right," I said.

"Let's go, Max," Cody added.

We inhaled the rest of our cereal and hurried out the door.

"I'll get the coffee cans," Cody said. "You grab the shovels."

He stopped and shook his finger at me. "And stay away from Mommy's tulips this time. Remember how much they cost?"

I frowned. "And just how was I supposed to

know tulips died so easy? They were only out of the ground for a few days."

The sun crept over the trees as we walked across the yard. I chose a spot away from Cody and away from the flowers. Birthday Miracle scampered over and joined me.

"I'm a good hole-digger, puppy," I said. I shoveled a clump of dirt and tossed it to the side. This is almost like being at the beach, I thought. Except I don't have to worry about pinchy crabs. Worms don't even have claws or arms for that matter. Wait. What about teeth?

"Worms don't bite, do they, Cody?"

"No," he said. "But snakes do."

I froze, then slowly searched the area. "Snakes?"

Cody grinned. "Ooh," he said. "There's one right there."

I sprang to my feet and spun around in a circle. "Where?"

He stuffed his hand in the hole and pulled out a pink wiggly worm.

"Right here." He held the worm high in the air. It squirmed in the sunlight.

"Oh," I said. "A worm."

"There's another one," Cody said. Every scoop seemed to uncover more.

I looked down at my empty hole. "I haven't found one yet," I said.

"Just keep digging."

I jammed the shovel into the dirt and pried a clod loose. Something moved.

"Ah-ha," I said. I stuck my finger in the hole, but the pink nub vanished.

That sneaky worm must have had an escape tunnel built in! I wondered what room his tunnel led to.

"Cody, do worms have houses like us?"

"No, I think they're just holes."

I picked more dirt away and unearthed a single worm. I knew what room I'd hide in if some giant was wrecking my house.

"Yuck, it looks like he was in the bathroom." I wiped some worm goo on my shorts.

I held him close to my face for a good look. "I'll call you Gerald," I said. "You look like a Gerald to me."

I plopped him in the can and went back to work. My next shovel hit the jackpot. Five worms tumbled out.

"Whoa," I said. "It's a wiggly worm party!" I dropped them into the can one by one.

"There you go, Francesca. See you later, Melvin

and Alphonso. Enjoy your new home, Larry. In you go, Bernice."

A shadow appeared over my can. I looked up.

"Bernice?" Cody said.

"Uh-huh, that's one of my worms."

Cody stared at me for a second, then shrugged his shoulders.

"I think we have enough," he said. "Let's go in."

"Okay, just one more," I jabbed the shovel into the ground and pulled out a clump of dirt. I rolled it over in time to see a big worm sneak back into a hole.

"Come out of there, Sammy," I said to the worm. She looked like a Sammy to me. Just then, Birthday Miracle ran by and stole the clod of dirt.

"Hey!" I said. "Sammy is in there."

She tore off across the yard. I sprinted after her, but I couldn't catch up.

She stopped near the back door and crunched on the glob of dirt. Poor Sammy, I thought. I crept slowly toward Birthday Miracle and lunged at her right when Daddy opened the door, clutching a big bag of trash. Birthday Miracle scurried between his legs and into the house.

"Watch out, Daddy!" I said. "She's got Sammy!"

"Whoa, whoa!" he said. "Not with those shoes on. They're filthy and I just finished cleaning."

He dangled the foul-smelling bag in front of me.

I fumbled to undo my laces. Mommy's scream stopped me dead in my tracks.

Daddy looked at me. "And what exactly is a Sammy?"

Chapter 4

A New White Rag

"A WORM," I said.

The muddy paw prints led to Mommy's room. I almost tripped over Birthday Miracle as I flew through the door. That's when I saw the clod lying in the laundry basket. It was right on top of Mommy's favorite sundress—the white one.

"I'll clean it up, Mommy." I said. "I swear!"

I plucked the slimy blob from the basket and stuffed it in my pocket, then went to work on the stain. I rubbed it with my shirt.

"It's getting lighter," I said.

"Don't!" she said. "You'll only make it worse."

I stopped. The blotch was definitely lighter, but it was also definitely bigger.

"Please, just put it down."

She buried her head in her hands.

Daddy poked his head in. "Uh, is everything all right in here?"

Mommy peeked at him through her fingers and pointed to the laundry.

"Oh," he said. "Just had to be the white one, didn't it?"

Mommy nodded, but didn't say a word.

"Okay, Max," he said. "You should go help Cody pack the truck now. I'll be out in a minute."

I gently laid the dress down. "I'm sorry, Mommy. I was just trying to help."

"I know, Max," she said. "Good luck today. I know you'll have a great time."

I went to help Cody and Daddy joined us a few minutes later.

"Well," he said, starting the truck. "The good news is the floor is clean, again."

"And the bad news?" I asked.

"Dresses make expensive rags."

Cody elbowed me. "Nice going."

"It's only a dress," Daddy said.

I knew he was trying to make me feel better. He winked at me in the mirror and we were on our way. We pulled up to the edge of a towering forest after we'd heard only a few songs.

"Wait just a second," I said. "Where's the water? You can't fish in trees."

Daddy pointed to a clearing in the brush. "See that path?"

Cody and I searched the tree line.

"It leads to the pond," he said.

We grabbed our gear and headed for the woods.

"Now let's stay together, boys," Daddy said. "It's easy to get turned around out here."

We tromped down the trail and Daddy told us more tales about Toothy Brutus. We grew more excited with every step.

"I can't wait any longer," Cody said. "Race you?"

I didn't even give him an answer. I just took off down the path.

"Oh no, you don't," he said. He whizzed past me and almost knocked me over.

I ran my fastest, but it was no use. I knew I'd never be able to beat Cody in a fair race. That's when I spotted a bend in the trail up ahead. That bend was my chance to win.

I leapt off the trail into the thick brush. The leaves crunched as I ran into the woods. I ran a while, looking for the path, but I didn't see it.

I slowed to catch my breath after a few more steps. "Hmm," I said, turning around. "Maybe it's this way." I walked a few feet. "No, that's not it."

It might be time to go back, I thought. I turned around, but couldn't find the way. All the nature looked exactly the same!

I climbed onto a log and stood on my tippy-toes. "Nope," I said. "Just more trees."

The woods were quiet now and I felt alone.

"Okay, Max," I said to myself. "Take it easy." I sat down on the log and opened my pack.

"Let's see. I've got some cheddar cheese popcorn, a bottle of water, and a bag of carrot sticks." A sinking feeling came over me and my cheeks felt hot.

"I'm going to starve to death out here! There won't be anything left but a pile of bones and some carrot sticks."

Think. How can I get out of this one? I rubbed my hands back and forth on my legs. I felt a lump in my pocket.

"Of course," I said. "That's it!"

CHAPTER 5

The Longcut

"MY WHISTLE!" I jammed my hand into my pocket, but jerked it right back out. Something squishy was moving in there. "My shorts are alive!"

I pulled the shorts off and shook them so I could see what exactly was living in my pocket. Out tumbled my muddy whistle, with Sammy tangled around it!

"Sammy. I forgot you were in there." I plopped her into my tin can and tried the whistle.

Ptfff. Ptfff.

It was clogged with dirt. I spat out the grit and tried again, but it was no use.

Great. What now? I sat on a log and rubbed my shirt, wishing I'd brought Fuzzy.

That's when I heard leaves crackling in the distance. I couldn't tell who or what it was, but it was

getting closer. I gathered my things and was about
to take off when I heard a faint voice.

"Ma-ax!" It was coming from the direction of
the rustling leaves.

"Ma-ax! Where are you?"

It was Cody!

"Over here!" I screamed. "I'm lost in
the wilderness."

Cody appeared from behind a tree. "There you
are," he said.

I flung my arms around him and squeezed.

"Okay, okay," he said prying me off. "Enough already."

He stepped back and looked me up and down. "Why are you in your undies?"

I could feel my cheeks get red.

"My shorts were alive, but it was only Sammy."

He rubbed my head. "Put your clothes on. The pond is right over there."

We walked to the clearing where Daddy was setting up our poles.

"I thought I told you to stay on the trail, Max," Daddy said.

I smiled. "I took a shortcut during our race. It turned out to be more of a longcut."

"Well," he said, "I guess no harm done."

He handed a pole to Cody, who quickly put on a worm and cast it perfectly on the first try.

Plunk.

The bobber landed with a splash and floated on the surface.

"Is my pole baited?" I asked. "I'm ready to fish."

Daddy handed me the rod.

I looked at it and frowned. "Hey," I said, "where's the hook?"

"About that," he said. "You need to practice a few times without one."

Daddy rubbed the back of his head. "We don't want a repeat performance of our last trip, do we?"

"You're right," I said. "Who knew hooks were so hard to get out of necks?"

"Remember to hold the button on the reel."

He took a few steps back and gave me the nod.

Swish.

The pole cut through the air. I waited, searching for the bobber, but I couldn't find it.

Daddy chuckled behind me. I turned and spotted it lying on the ground in a tangle of line.

"I think you let go too early," said Daddy. "Keep your finger on the button until the pole is pointing at the water."

"Got it," I said.

"Watch," said Cody, launching his bobber with perfect form.

Plunk.

"Bull's-eye," Cody said.

"Show-off," I said. "I'll catch the biggest fish, just you wait."

"Try again," said Daddy. "It takes practice."

I swung the pole with all my might.

Swish.

"A-hem," Daddy gestured toward Cody.

My bobber had made it to the water this time, but it was tangled around Cody's line.

"Hey," he said, "I'm fishing over here."

Daddy reached for my pole. "Better," he said. "At least it's in the water."

Bloop. Bloop.

We all stood still, listening.

"Did you hear that?" said Cody.

"What was it?" I asked.

Daddy pointed to the pond.

There were a few small rings on the glassy surface.

"What?" I said. "There's nothing there."

"Exactly," said Cody. "Where's my bobber?"

Chapter 6

Freedom!

"THE LINES ARE tangled," Cody said.

"Hold on just a second." Daddy looped my pole around Cody's a few times and just like that, we were free!

"Something's on my hook!" Cody said.

His rod tip twitched as he cranked.

"I can feel it pulling," he said.

I stepped closer for a better look.

"Take your time," Daddy said. "You don't want to snap it."

Cody bit the corner of his lip. The line danced in the dark water.

Bloop.

"There's the bobber," I said.

It appeared in a swirl next to his feet.

"Just a few more turns," Daddy said.

"There it is," said Cody. He was so excited he almost dropped the reel. The fish flopped in the shallow water.

"It has spots!" I said. "What is it?"

"Trout," said Cody. "Rainbow trout." He stepped back and lifted his pole. It dangled from the glistening line.

"Wow," I said.

"It's a beauty," said Daddy.

Cody slid his hand down the line and the trout flipped right off the hook. Cody froze then slowly bent down.

"No," said Cody. "My fish!"

It seemed to hover motionless in the water. Nothing moved except its gills opening and closing.

He worked so hard, I thought.

Cody lunged forward and snatched the fish right out of the water before it could escape.

Splash!

"You're not getting away from me!" he said.

Seconds later, I watched in awe as Cody strolled up the bank firmly clutching the trout.

"I got you," he said.

"I thought you lost that one," Daddy said. "That was amazing."

"Yeah," I said. "The coolest thing I've seen all day."

"Put him on the stringer," Daddy said.

I grabbed my pole and leapt in the air.

"Daddy, I need a hook! I want to catch the next one."

Cody put on fresh bait and cast his line back to the same spot.

"Hurry up, Max," he said. "There's more where that came from."

I held the rod while Daddy tied the hook. "There you go, Max. All you need now is bait."

I rooted around in my can until I found Sammy.

"You're my special worm," I whispered. I carefully balanced her on the hook, careful not to poke her.

Swish.

Plunk.

"Look!" I said. "It's actually in the water and no tangles."

Daddy snickered behind me. "I don't think you're going to catch anything."

"What?" I said. "That cast was perfect. And look, Cody's bobber is moving again."

Cody yanked back on his pole and started reeling.

"Yes," Daddy said. "Your bobber made it out, but..."

He tapped his foot on the ground. There was Sammy, squiggling in the dirt.

"I don't understand," I said. "Cody's worms aren't falling off."

I handed Sammy over and she wiggled nervously in Daddy's hand.

"Max, maybe we shouldn't name the bait," he said. "You have to put the hook through the worm or it won't stay on."

He moved the hook closer and almost touched her with it!

My heart sunk. "Wait, you want me to shish-ke-bab her?!" I screamed. "You want me to stab Sammy?!"

Daddy raised his eyebrows.

"Well, I guess that's one way to look at it," he said.

"Shish-ke-Sammy is the only way?"

Daddy chuckled. "That's what you have to do if you want the bait to stay on."

"No way." I stomped my foot and grabbed Sammy. "I won't do it."

I dug into my can and produced a handful of wiggly worms. I pointed to each one.

"That's Gerald. This is Francesca and that's Alphonso. Over here are Larry, Melvin, and Bernice."

"Alphonso won't catch any fish as long as he's in the can," Daddy said.

I stuffed them back in and grabbed my gear. Then I ran over to Cody.

"Worm-killer!" I shouted and grabbed his can of bait.

"I'm going to set you free!" I shrieked and headed for the trail.

Cody passed his jiggling pole to Daddy and took off after me.

"Hey!" he shouted. "Come back here with my bait!"

CHAPTER 7

Cheddar Cheese Popcorn

AS I SPRINTED down the trail, I could hear Cody panting behind me. He was closing in. My lungs burned and my gear was slowing me down.

"Get back here, Max!" he shouted. "That's my bait."

"Freedom for the wiggly worms!" I said.

He was gaining, but how close was he? I glanced over my shoulder just as he reached for my shirt.

Gak.

Uggh.

I dropped everything when I hit the ground. I could see streaks of blue sky between the tree tops.

"Ouch," I said, rubbing my neck. "You almost took my head off."

Cody frowned and scooped up some of the wiggling mound of worms.

"I'm sorry, but you stole my bait and the fish are biting."

"I didn't know we were going to stab them."

Cody shook his head. "Don't you want to catch Toothy Brutus?"

"Not if it means sticking a hook through Sammy, or stabbing Francesca."

"Suit yourself."

He turned and started back down the path. "Good luck catching him with no bait."

I brushed myself off, gathered my stuff, and picked up the rest of the worms.

"It's okay, little guys," I said. "No hooks for you."

I dug a small hole and dumped them in.

"There you go."

I patted the squiggling mound of dirt.

Growl.

I rubbed my stomach. "I think it's time for that cheddar cheese popcorn."

I popped open the bag and stuffed a handful in my mouth.

"Mmm," I said, "that is good." I thought about Toothy Brutus as I crunched. A few kernels fell to the ground, so I kicked them into the water. That's when a flash of color caught my eye.

Quack. Quack.

A duck was paddling by pretty close to shore.

"Hey there, little duck. I bet you like popcorn."

I hurled a piece into the water. The duck gobbled it up.

"I know. It's good, right?"

I tossed a few more in and he gulped those down too.

Snap! Snap!

Flap-flap-flap.

"Wait, you forgot some!"

The water churned where the duck had been and the last few kernels bobbed about.

"I wonder what scared him."

I watched the popcorn as the water calmed. There were five soggy pieces.

Snap! Snap!

The water rippled and I strained my eyes to see. I think there were three left now.

Snap!

No, two.

"Wait a minute!" I said. "Something else likes cheddar cheese popcorn."

Snap!

The floating popcorn was disappearing one piece at a time.

I grabbed my pole and fumbled with the hook and bobber. I stuck on two pieces of my cheddar cheese bait. Okay, Max. You can do this. Just remember to hold the button. I stepped to the bank and slung the pole over my shoulder.

Swish.

Plunk.

It landed smack in the middle of the rippling water.

"Direct hit."

My hands trembled. I tried to swallow, but the lump in my throat wouldn't let me. Everything was still, except for my beating heart.

Snap!

CHAPTER 8

Epic Battle

THE BOBBER AND popcorn were gone. All I could hear was the reel spinning. And it was spinning fast!

Zzzzz…..Zzzzz….Zzzzzz!

The pole bent as the line peeled into the pond. Could this be Toothy Brutus? Could it really be him?

I stumbled forward, hanging on with all my might, to the very edge of the pond. The water leaked in through the toes of my shoes.

A wave of panic came over me as the thought of being dragged in filled my mind.

"My whistle," I said. "It's still in my pocket."

I knew I'd drop the pole for sure if I tried to get it.

"Help!" I screamed. "I got Toothy Brutus!"

I dug my heels into the muddy bank and trudged back onto dry land. I didn't know what to do.

"Dad-dy! Co-dy!" I yelled into the woods. It was no use. They couldn't hear me.

I took one hand off the pole and stuffed it in my pocket. The knuckles on my other hand were white as I dug my fingernails into the pole.

"Finally!" I pulled out the whistle and stuck it in my mouth. I blew it with everything I had.

My ears popped and I saw stars, but there was no sound. I rocked back on my heels and stumbled forward. Worm dirt. It was clogged with worm dirt!

I loosened my grip and dropped the pole. It skipped across the ground and was headed for the water.

"No!"

At that same moment, something moved beside me. I saw a blur out of the corner of my eye. It was Cody! He dove for the rod just before it slipped into the pond.

"I got it," he said, lifting it out of the muck.

"Are you all right, Max?" Daddy asked.

The reel continued to zing.

"I think it's Toothy Brutus," I said.

Cody handed me the pole. "He's your fish. Reel him in."

"Easy does it," Daddy said.

Click. Click. Click.

I slowly cranked the reel.

"Hey," I said. "It's coming in."

Without warning, the tip twitched and then the entire rod jerked wildly.

"There he goes again," Daddy said. "Hold on, Max."

"I am," I said.

I sloshed into the water. It was pulling me in!

"Cody," I said, "what do I do?"

Cody grabbed me by the waist. "Don't worry, I got you."

Snap!

The pole went limp and the line trailed off into the pond. We stood in silence. I didn't know silence could be so loud.

Tears welled in my eyes. I rubbed them and buried my head in Cody's shoulder.

"He's gone," I said softly. "I lost him."

He squeezed me and swung me around in the air.

"Are you kidding me?" he said. "You came so close."

"And you did it all by yourself," added Daddy.

I wiped the tears with my shirt.

"But I really wanted to see him," I said. "I didn't want to keep him."

"I know," Daddy said. "But what a terrific story."

"Question," Cody said. "If you didn't use worms, how did you catch him?"

I held up the mostly eaten bag of popcorn and tossed a handful into the water.

"Cheddar cheese popcorn," I said. "I'm not the only one who loves this stuff."

"Huh," Daddy said. "Never would have guessed."

He looked at his watch.

"Can't we stay just five more minutes?" I asked.

Snap!

"Not funny, Cody," I said. "I know I lost him, but you don't have to tease me."

Snap!

"It's not me, Max," he said. "Look."

He pointed to the pond.

Snap! Snap!

We all watched as the last few kernels were snatched from the surface.

"I told you," I said.

Daddy fidgeted with his pole. He searched for popcorn to bait his hook.

I tugged on his shirt. "I don't think you're going to need that." I pointed to the shadow approaching in the dark water.

Snap!

I tossed another handful in, a few pieces landed on shore.

Snap!

A huge head with two beady eyes emerged from the murky pond. He looked right at me.

Snap! Snap!

"It's a turtle!" I screamed. "Toothy Brutus is a turtle!"

"Whoa!" Cody said. "Do snapping turtles get that big?"

Daddy pressed his hands against our chests and forced us back. "Give him some space, boys. That's one giant snapper."

Toothy Brutus scooched the front half of his body onto the bank. He had eaten all the popcorn and was looking for more.

I emptied the bag on the ground beside him.

Snap! Snap!

He devoured it all.

We stood watching the massive creature enjoy his cheddar cheese popcorn. When the pile was gone, he slid back into the cool pond and vanished.

The walk back to the car was quiet. I wondered about Toothy Brutus and what he was doing. I could tell we were all thinking about him.

Daddy was the first to break the silence. "Nobody's ever going to believe us," he said. "Cheddar cheese popcorn."

"That's okay," Cody said. "We all saw it."

"Together," I said.

"Oh, Max," Cody said. "I almost forgot." He reached into his pack and handed me his can of bait. "We didn't use these little guys. You can have them."

I smiled and took the can.

"Freedom for more wiggly worms," I whispered.

I ran up ahead to dig them a new home. And this time, I made sure to stay on the trail.

FROM THE AUTHOR

If you enjoyed this book, please leave an honest review. Word-of-mouth is truly powerful, and your words will make a huge difference. Thank you.

As you read this, I'm writing the next Max E. James adventure. For updates on new releases, promotions, and other great children's book recommendations, join my Kids' Club at:

http://www.maxejames.com/kids-club/

DON'T FORGET YOUR FREE DOWNLOAD

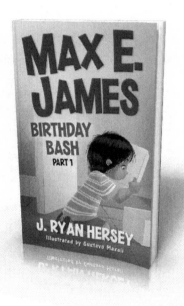

Type the link below into your browser to get started.
http://eepurl.com/cfcfkj

About the Author

J. Ryan Hersey is a devoted father and husband who lives in beautiful Hampton Roads, Virginia. His stories are inspired by the adventures he shares with his wife and two boys. He is author of the Max E. James children's series. To find out more or connect with him directly, visit his website at:

http://www.maxejames.com

About the Illustrator

Gustavo Mazali lives with his family in beautiful Buenos Aires, Argentina. Having drawn all his life, Gustavo has developed the unique ability to capture the essence of children in his art. You can view his portfolio at:

http://www.mazali.com

About the Editor

Amy Betz founded Tiny Tales Editing after working as a children's book editor at several major publishing houses. She lives with her family in Bethel, Connecticut. You can learn more about Amy at:
http://www.tinytalesediting.com

All Titles

Beach Bound
Birthday Bash: Part 1
Birthday Bash: Part 2
Fishing Fever

52409305R00037

Made in the USA
San Bernardino, CA
07 September 2019